The Publisher

I0742347

Also by Ray Clift and published by Ginninderra Press

Fiction

The Journey of Hamlyn Baylis Wells

Always In Denial

Smithy's Cupboard

Shaken & Stirred

Shalom Samuel

The Last Journey of Hamlin Baylis Wells

She Walks the Line

The Journeys of Hamlin Baylis Wells

Smithy & Suzie

Three in One

Non-fiction

Maybe Blue Ghosts

It's a Fine Line

Cops, Crooks, Courts & Spooks

Ray Clift

The Publisher

Thanks to

my family

Sharon Kernot

Gary MacRae

Stephen and Brenda Matthews of Ginninderra Press

The Publisher
ISBN 978 1 76041 152 7
Copyright text © Ray Clift 2016
Copyright cover image © Kevin Penhallow – Fotolia.com

First published 2016 by
GINNINDERRA PRESS
PO Box 3461 Port Adelaide SA 5015
www.ginninderrapress.com.au

Contents

1

Geelong

1999

'Why are you angry?'

My third wife asks me that every morning, usually at breakfast, when my face is still pale and wan from restless sleep. The death stare comes on my face, which has no effect on her after fifteen years of togetherness. I sigh loud enough to wake up Bouncer from his dream of bones and he stares into my face. His tail wags slightly

'I'm not angry,' I say. 'It's just my face.'

I've spruiked those lines at least a dozen times. I'm happy enough with her but after all that time she has to learn that I don't talk in the morning, which is rough on her. Jackie's full of lively chatter bubbling away like a soda water siphon. I guess that's one of the reasons we got together. Another reason is that she's a great creator of illustrations for children's books.

The small round shell-framed mirror is clamped on top of the computer with a rickety bracket in need of repair. It frames my face and sometimes when I work I study my image.

I certainly *look* angry. The fact is that I *am* angry, most mornings. I wake up angry. Still.

'Don't you know that everyone is afraid of you?' Her words purr out with a gentle but positive tone. 'You're intimidating. You weren't like that once.'

'Bullshit.'

'Ask your kids. And mine for that matter.' She had added two great blonde, grown-up stepkids to make up our brood once we became lovers. 'Them too, Edgar.'

'Them too what?'

'Afraid of you.'

I stand up and take my old coffee mug out to the kitchen and run the hot water tap. I wash the cup. I wipe it and put it on the top laminated shelves of the cupboard. Everything must have a place.

I trip on the way to the computer. 'Damn cats,' I mutter, 'always playing with my footwear,' though it might have been a balance thing because of my Ménière's disease, or just age.

The coffee spills over the carpet. Jackie rushes out with a cloth and mops it up. She knows that I'm likely to fly off the handle.

I choose to sit outside for a while and stop my racing thoughts. Thoughts which flash back to secondary school, when praise would come in bucket loads about my composition, spelling, dictation and spelling. About the time when the headmaster, Mr Selby-Jones, cornered me for a quick chat. The words he said had a strong influence in my life.

'Your English skills are excellent, young Edgar. You're bound for a career in literature.'

I smiled.

He turned back and said, 'Give my regards to your dad.'

I found out later that he had served in the army with Dad.

But in spite of his praise, my heart was set on a naval career. How could I have guessed at that young age that the events which were to flow from my short career in the navy would be a stepping stone into working for publishing company? I allow myself a smile when I think about that later career. It really came down to connections and of course some weeks of lessons about writing and editing.

I still can recall my expectation of what the inside of a publishing company would look like. I imagined oak-panelled walls, shag carpets and big-busted secretaries racing around. In fact, the receptionist wore black, chain-smoked and had photos of her grandkids on her desk, and there were dull abstract paintings hanging in the lobby

I take a last puff of my cigar, butt it out and shuffle back inside.

The computer begs and I sit there thinking about the little bit of tension which springs up like weeds in June on some mornings and realise how practised I have become at concealing anger when I need to. It's all to do with my past jobs and the publishing company which I own, and which is starting to show some ragged edges around the very old beloved bookshelves, which I would be loath to part with: I could afford to get a make-over with the furniture because I now occupy the office built on the back of the old family home, which my parents bequeathed to me.

But my sly attempts to conceal my anger are starting to show through of late. I'm sixty-four and recently found that I could enjoy life without being constantly surrounded by frantic new authors, most of whom don't bother to follow the easy rules on my website for unpublished manuscript submissions.

I'm learning not to worry about what people think. What I'm angry about is simply mortality brought on by a particle of asbestos having a great time dashing around in my lungs. A legacy of my old ship in the navy – years ago, I might add.

I've spent a lot of years struggling to be Mr Nice Guy and I've never really made it. Now my true self is shining through. I am Captain Grumpy or sourpuss, yet when I smile, the scowl just fades away and it surprises all who witness it.

The small mirror, though, is a worry now, and the image changes. There he is: my father. I'm beginning to look like him. I look away. I look back. He's still there. But it's not only Dad who is in my mirror. There is Commander Bartholomew-Smith, my skipper from the HMAS *Sydney III*, whose sole mission in life was to place me into misery until I'd leave the senior service either through conduct unbecoming, or just through simple resignation.

It is said that names will never hurt you. I beg to differ. Bartholomew-

Smith altered my destiny. My tracks were shaped into a fashion which anybody who knew me could imagine. I was like a lamb to the slaughter.

The admiral came aboard for a short time, just before Bart, as was one of his nicknames, boarded. The admiral was an old hand and it appeared to me that he was well liked by all ranks. More important was that he remembered names and what our backgrounds were.

'I see that you won a few matches in your boxing career, before and after you joined us. How is that going?'

'I had some concussion and I'm advised to lay off for a time. But I still train, sir – mainly skipping.'

He stared at me with a look which was hard to fathom. Maybe he knew something that I didn't and it puzzled me for a time, until my thoughts were diverted by other pressing duties.

'How are you finding being in charge of men who were once your bosses when you were a snotty?' he asked, using the nickname for a midshipman.

'It's okay, sir. I do more listening than talking, which seems to work out.'

'Fine. Fine, lad, and that is exactly the strategy I employed when I was as a young subby…so many years ago. So many friends killed in battle. So many drank themselves to death because of the horrors they had seen. You know, I used to think that metal wouldn't burn. How wrong was that?'

It appeared that he was unloading and found a friendly face who would listen to his take on the inner demons which he had, still floating about. He reminded me a bit of Dad and I warmed to him in those few precious seconds.

2

Hoover

Hoover, that was my nickname on board the ship in 1955. It started out benignly, as anyone might guess, from the initials which I shared with the famous FBI boss J. Edgar Hoover, but within a short space of time it became a symbol of derision. I was living on a ship of shame, with no escape.

I tried with all my might, and Dad's advice, to be a good officer. I treated the men under me with care and concern and saw that they carried out their tasks as efficiently as possible. I maintained a clean presentation in my cabin and in appearance, and I was of course very punctual. But it was to no avail. I was also aware of my younger age and junior rank, so I walked carefully, trying too hard to be Mr Nice Guy, which I hadn't always been before the navy

News travels fast on ship, even one with a couple of thousand sailors. Even on a flagship which is entitled to have an admiral on board. There's a good chance, with a crew that large, that one might never meet the same rating twice. God knows what it must be like on a cramped submarine – the tale was that it was a federal offence to fart in a sub. And then there were the cabin boy jokes. The one I remember came from the mouth of an old stoker. 'It's not wine, women and song once we're three months out. It's rum, bum and gramophone.' And judging by the looks he gave the young midshipmen, I reckon I knew which he would prefer.

I found myself on double shifts, like four hours on and four hours off, which were only worked when in action stations. As a result of that tiring load, I was starting to drop things. Like a cup of steaming cocoa which was dropped at the feet of the commander whose eyes did not show peace and comfort to one of his junior officers.

'Get a rag and mop it up now, Mr Williams,' he barked and I ran around, crazy like, trying to find a rag.

I went past an old petty officer who must have had some pity for me because he shoved a rag into my hand, and then shot through like a Bondi tram, lest he be caught helping the hated junior man.

The word had got around. I was to be isolated, reduced, traduced and pushed out of the way – or worse, out of the job, which I wanted to love and to stay in for thirty years. Be honourable and respected, just like my dad, the hero.

The eleventh commandment – don't get caught. And, the old hands added, if caught, do not admit it; if asked who else was involved, act dumb; and – best of all – I wasn't there and I didn't do it.

My only sin was to be caught.

Most sailors are careful not to be caught masturbating yet it was rife on board the ship – everyone was doing it from what I saw and heard in the night. It was almost a hanging offence to be gay. And some of the cooks were. But no one touched the protected cooks, because you might end up with a couple of boot tacks in the gravy or a bit of green goosy, just delivered from the galley, in amongst the custard. As to the gays, I certainly had an offer to join a circle, but the thought of even kissing a man repulsed me.

Hypocrisy reigned.

In one mad impulsive moment after getting up with a huge erection, I grabbed a small portable vacuum cleaner which I used to keep dandruff off the blue uniform. I shoved it on the end of my member and stood watching in the mirror, stark naked, while it hummed away steadily. The urge was just near being sated, with my eyes half closed, and on the verge of ejaculation, when I heard a cough from behind.

There was the steward standing at the open doorway holding a drink tray. His lips were held tight as a dead man; he was controlling a burst of laughter. I couldn't stop the groaning little love machine, which rumbled on, detached from its mate.

I threw it in the sink and yelled, 'Get out.'

And I guessed that the little crawler would be at full gallop to the bridge, excited and blurting out what he had seen to the commander, who would be rubbing his hands in glee within a micro-second.

I was due up on the bridge. My face had drained of colour. I brushed my cheeks. A straight back and a hat on straight. I was ready to face the music and I walked carefully with controlled breathing up to the bridge. I felt a lot of eyes staring at me I thought of former navy men who faced execution and I wondered how they had reacted. But this fellow was not a compassionate Billy Budd captain.

I took my place behind the man, who was busy staring out to sea through his binoculars. He put them down and turned round slowly. I saluted him but he did not return it. The messenger of doom whispered into one of the officer's ears and they both chuckled, as did the remainder of the men at their duties. I waited. The silence was incredible in spite of all the machinery rumbling away.

He turned back and studied my face and I knew I was raw meat. He picked up his cup of steaming cocoa and stirred it with a spoon. He stared at me as if I were a cigarette stub, or an empty chair, just something in his line of vision, without interest – a bug to be squashed. Like Captain Bligh versus Fletcher Christian.

He leaned back and grinned again, exposing his protruding yellowed teeth and then spoke. 'So, Mr Williams, how do we address you now?' He clicked his fingers, which was a habit I had noticed, and gazed at the roof.

I thought then, he's a wanker. I'm only part time – just learning the craft.

He looked around at the gathering crew. He was milking his audience just like a stand-up comedian, and then he spun back to me. 'I know, let's call you Hoover. Isn't that appropriate?'

I didn't answer. It was his show.

'Cat got your tongue?'

I could feel the anger rising in me. The men were now laughing out loud and he was waving his arms like a bandsman encouraging his band, and I thought, if ever there comes a time when the stars are aligned, I'll make you pay, mate.

I mustered up courage and replied, 'Well what do you want me to say?' No sir at the end.

'Extra duties for you. I'll tell the cook to put some extra bromide in your tucker just to slow you down.'

I didn't speak but he had to have an add-on just for the entertainment of the troops.

'Perhaps we ought to have a wedding. What say, sailors?' He turned back, with the teeth almost about to burst out of his mouth. His eyes bolting, just like a surprised meerkat.

'Mr Williams is married to his comrade – Miss Hoover. What say we?' He was running out of lines and again he prodded me with a 'Well?'

'Get fucked.' This time I added, 'Sir.'

I about-turned and strolled away with him yelling out, 'Get the Crushers,' the nickname of the naval police. 'He's going to the brig.'

But that was not the end because I found out within a few days, when my grub was shoved under the cell door, what he had planned for me when we reached the equator: he would scrub the charge of insolence if I fought big Jim the chief coxswain, who had a fearful reputation. He was about two stone heavier than me and around six-four as opposed to my five-eleven.

I started to exercise in the cell with bar chins, push-ups, sit-ups and squats, and running on the spot. I would be ready in spite of the mismatch, which by now was causing some consternation with the other officers, who secretly couldn't stand the bully Bart.

*

The ring on the flight deck was set up in the calm waters of the equator.

I strolled out in my dressing gown and stood in my corner with an officer who I had befriended, awaiting the arrival of Black Bart.

Dan rubbed my shoulders and put on the gloves. He bandaged my hands just before the announcement of who would punch who. 'Look, Big Jim's out of condition but keep out of reach of that left of his. Dance about, get him to breathe heavily. I reckon he'll stumble. Go in then, right into his midriff, and rain some punches to his eyes. His eyesight isn't that good.'

Big Jim came in and I saw Black Bart stand alongside the admiral. This was his time to finish me off but I wasn't afraid of some bruises.

The bell rang and we moved into the centre and shook hands. Big Jim had a look of sympathy of his face. The PT instructor told us to make it a clean fight and the bell rang again. Sailors were exchanging money and I bet it was on me losing. I had news for them. Still, it would not be easy.

The first round was a virtual stand-off. I had to watch when he got in close with clinches, trying to kidney punch. I backed and hit him in the stomach and danced around until the bell rang.

'Watch him in those clinches, keep out of his reach. He's breathing hard now.'

I danced out and he kept trying to corner me on the ropes with pushes. He caught me on the chin with a right, which caused me to stagger. I shook my head clear and went right in under his guard, and hit him twice in the stomach, and landed one on his right ear. He staggered on one leg. Then I pounded him with punch after punch. His eyes rolled back and blood fell from his ear.

The bell rang and after a few minutes his trainer chucked in the towel. My hand was held up as the winner. The crowd roared.

The admiral stepped out and came into the ring and shook my hand. 'Well done, lad.'

But Bart was nowhere to be seen and I guessed he'd hoped that my presumed weak state in the brig would have gone against me. He had been wrong.

There was more good news. Bart had to fly home for a family death and by the time he was once again on the ship I was in Korea, seconded for two weeks to help the base signals section. I did not see him again in the service.

I had some big thinking to do about my navy career. I was still a one-ringer and other, more junior men had been promoted above me.

3

Family Life

We weren't stuck for money when I was born in 1935, which was surprising at the end of the Depression. I was educated at the prestigious Geelong Grammar School, which had been Dad's school as well. He had been the class captain and the dux of his class; I had big shoes to fill.

The war came. Dad was already a reserve officer with the engineering corps and by 1941 he was in the Middle East, in the thick of it.

Mum helped with the usual war effort and at times I boarded at the school. The school was all about strict discipline in class and on the sports fields. Mum sent Dad a copy of my latest results with the exams. He returned a letter addressed to me. 'Keep it up, lad – well done.' That was gold for me. I don't recall any other favourable remarks from that time. Unlike other fathers at the school, he never had a cane. One word from him was enough.

When I recalled Bible studies at school, Dad reminded me of Moses coming down from the mountain. When he spoke, all heads flicked around. All mouths were shut while people listened to the words from God – for a while, anyway.

He was a company commander at Tobruk when a mortar round messed up his leg. He was sent home and never returned to the conflict. Mum welcomed him back with those voluptuous arms and within a few days he was back at his old desk as an architect with a well known firm. The office was sprinkled with many old World War I veterans, some with missing legs and arms and some still coughing from the effects of the gas. With his old buddies, his job became his life outside of us, and at times we did not see much of him, due to his long shifts and the RSL club. I guess it was his escape from the horrors.

My sister Joan was much older than me and through the lonely years was a constant companion for my mum Doreen. Joan married another soldier not long after Dad came home and by all accounts they were happy enough, though she lived in a lot of army houses around the country. I did not see much of her after that.

Mabel, a big-breasted war widow, took a shine to me when I offered to cut her lawns for a bit of pocket money, but there were a few strings attached.

I remember the scene very well. When she pushed me into her wood shed, when she undid my fly buttons and out it popped looking for trouble. She grabbed me and started to massage it and it was all over in seconds. It was gone, done and dusted and dribbling. There was shouting when Dad arrived, and she disappeared into the house.

I sat on the seat, out of earshot from Joan and Mum, when he sat opposite staring at me. He wasn't talking: just staring with those piercing Welsh hazel eyes (he reckoned that his ancestors were bowmen with Edward III at Crècy). I felt he could see right through me and that all of my secrets were printed along the inside of my spine.

My heart began to pound – thump, thump, thump – and the trees behind seemed to sway in time. I couldn't keep up the masquerade another minute and I had to speak. 'She pushed me into the woodshed and grabbed me on the cock. It all burst out in one sort of jerking minute, Dad.'

His normally stiff face softened. I didn't speak right then.

He leaned back and locked his hands behind his neck. A small grin came over his face and he spoke in hushed tones. 'It's OK, son. You're only fifteen. Mabel will be told to back off. Obviously she's lonely, being a widow, and you, a sprightly lad, became her target. Don't tell Mum about this and I don't think Joan knows. It's between you and me.'

My response was to scratch at my wet crotch, which was by then uncomfortable.

His steely hazel eyes returned as if they had been on a short holiday.

*

Dad's other life wasn't other women and I reckon it was because he would be hard pressed to find one whose care was better than my mum Doreen's.

He taught me the rudiments of boxing, which rounded off what I was learning at school. Though he didn't know much about baseball (which was my favourite sport), he certainly knew a lot about cricket and we all played together at home and on camping trips. Dad was a wizard with camps. Nothing was left to chance and he always ensured that we were always safe.

We sparred in the garage and I saw an opening, but it was blocked and then wham wham, his right hand came from nowhere onto my cheek. I flailed with my arms and we went into a bear hug until Dad broke it, with a quick push back and a yell.

'Whoa, whoa, whoa, lad.' And all the time holding the top of my head with his great long arms.

I saw another smile crease his face and it spoke a silent word.

I was not one to give up.

There were times when he would call out drill exercises from the kitchen window to me where I was either doing some weeding or throwing up my baseball. It was like I was a performing seal.

'All right, you, stand up straight, pull your belly in, pull your chin in, keep your shoulders back, hold your head level, look straight ahead, straight front, turn left, turn right, face the front, hold your hands out straight, palm down, palm up.' Then it was 'Pull your sleeves back.'

It finally stopped when the kettle whistled and Mum called out, 'Cuppa, love.'

'Yes, mate.' He always called her 'mate'.

*

The weekends were soon over and, interspersed with a dramatic turn of events, his other life of work resumed which occupied what spaces were available in his week of brilliant designs.

Mum told me on the quiet what the secret drama was about, once when I was home from boarding school, sporting a black eye after a bout which was pronounced a draw. Out came her treasured first aid kit and out came the pills, potions and creams. I sat watching her and the flabby arms which according to old relatives had been free of flab when she played basketball. And all the opposition got out of her way when those tree-stump thighs thundered down the court. Her arms were strong and I guessed there would be some triceps hiding there waiting to be released.

'Why are Dad's eyes so far off? They seem to be looking in a place miles away.'

She lowered her voice and spoke words which I now understood, due to the hygiene lessons at school – and what the smutty boys told me.

'His twin sister, your Auntie Doris – you haven't met her – is in a lunatic asylum.'

'What? The nut house?'

Mum gave me a clip across my ears.

'Ouch,' I whispered, wishing I had not spoken such indelicate words

'Right, Edgar, listen.'

I shut my mouth at her command. And waited for the secret to be revealed.

'She was raped. It was so bad that she never recovered. I don't think she has long for the planet. She has a growth.'

Back then, cancer was always called a growth.

Mum paused. 'Dad's burned up that the man, who's in Pentridge, is now able to study science and get a degree.'

I whispered 'Hell' to myself. Fancy crossing Dad, the war hero. I verbalised my thoughts of vengeance. 'Is he thinking how to get back at the bad man?'

Mum nodded.

I turned and saw fear welling in her eyes.

'I fear he'll pay someone to kill the man in gaol. Victor Marshall is as good as dead.'

I thought about this but had some other ideas: Dad is an upright man. I don't think he believes in God, though he spoke the word Amen in the Anglican church one day when I was near. Mum wouldn't go, because of her non-beliefs and the types of books she reads. She's a prolific reader and can knock over three giant novels in a week. It's no wonder I grew up with a love of books, with her reading out passages from suspense to romance. With all of that inside her head, I think she created a character, not unlike dad, who frees the maidens and kills the evil ones.

'Isn't Dad a freemason? I mean, they all help each other, don't they?' My question was carefully constructed to get the right answer.

But her response was cutting. 'Don't be cute, Edgar. I know what you're on about. No, whatever he's planned is on his shoulders – he won't involve friends.'

The conversation ended sharply and I was left pondering. Like, would my dad end up in gaol?

*

I was enrolled into the naval academy as a cadet. My life from that point was flat out, almost chaos, with so much to do to get the best marks possible in subjects and sport, and I was grateful for how much discipline Dad had instilled in me. I thought it would be a cakewalk, as they say nowadays.

I became the boxing champ for a time until I was severely concussed. Flinders Naval Depot provided the remainder of my chosen career as a signals officer and in 1955, after a graduation ceremony, which my parents attended, I was to be posted onto the flagship, the aircraft carrier HMAS *Sydney III*. Dad was there with all of his sparkling medals and, as he was a captain, many of the service people saluted him. I was overwhelmed with pride and couldn't wait for sea duties.

I looked at my one gold stripe and visualised how many more of those I would get after thirty years.

It went smoothly until Commander Bartholomew-Smith transferred to the ship. If I were to believe in reincarnation, then I would clearly state we must have been enemies in another life.

4

Job Interview

I made a firm decision (which would not have pleased Dad) to quit when I was ashore in Korea for some weeks, assisting the base signals crew. Six years was enough. The paperwork went through smoothly – surprise, surprise, because the process was usually lengthy. I had some leave and caught a plane back home and my reception from Dad was cool. I made a mental note to tell him what caused my big decision. I told Mum, and she was OK with it.

It was time to look for work and I was bound to find a job as an editor, if one was available. I did hear on the grapevine that Bart was shitty because he thought he could get rid of me. He apparently grumbled about my medal and checked up on it. Another miss for him, the loss of a whipping boy. He had made one big mistake the day after I was released from the brig. I was ordered to scrub his cabin floor. There on the bulkhead was a group school photo of when he attended the Geelong Boys Grammar School. He was at the back. My father the class captain was in the front row in the centre. I whistled and thought about it. My suffering under the tyrant was to do with payback. What happened between the two boys? I marked it for later on in life.

I worked up a lather sending away my résumé. I had some rejections but one of some promise came up. It was a fine firm in the heart of the CBD. I wore my best grey suit and the Geelong school tie and lugged along some material which they might want to peruse. There were to be two interviews, one with a panel and the other with the owner of the company.

There were many thoughts circling around in my head, so I nailed them all down, discarded the garbage and focused on what I might say to the panel. The interview with the senior partners was lengthy and many probing questions were asked. In my preparation the night before, I took some time to sandpaper some of the edges, evening out the rough spots in order to provide a smooth surface which a panel would be comfortable with, so that any awkward questions could easily slide past without much effort. I felt like a man who had fallen into a sandblaster and came out shiny and carbolic-scrubbed.

'Your preparation is almost perfect, Edgar,' one member of the panel said.

An air of anticipation hung in the atmosphere like a humid night before the wet season settled in for the long haul. A protracted silence followed as if they had a question hanging in the air – like, is he for real?

Another of the panel members broke the silence, pursuing my admission that two weeks ago I had not been sure how I would give my answers.

'How are you different now?'

I stalled for a quiet second. I smiled and looked him straight in the eyes. 'A lot less edgy,' I replied.

They shuffled their pens and papers and then nodded. I was told right then that I would have a final interview with the company director in a few days

*

I sat upright on the uncomfortable chair and watched as Leslie A. Banks perused my history. Armed with a yellow highlighter, he paused at times and marked some of the papers. The only sound came from a small whirring fan and some loud laughter in the editors' room. I noted his RSL badge, along with the blazing sun of an overseas service badge, both shining, with a refection cast upon the face of the badge from a flickering overhead light (which needed a new globe).

He looked up and smiled. 'Relax, Edgar. You're not with the

pussers now,' he said, using the nickname for sailors. 'Actually, I know your father very well and your lovely mum. He was my captain in the Middle East, until I transferred to Intelligence. How is he? I know he was badly wounded.'

'Good days and bad days, Mr Banks.'

'I'm pleased that he's coping. A lot don't. Give him my regards. I see you were a boxing champ at school and in the navy. Had any bouts lately?'

'A while back on the flight deck at the equator. I won.'

'That would have been a bit sweaty.'

I nodded, thinking, when will he get around to the nitty-gritty: do I get the job? I felt a bit like a man who had forgotten to tie his shoelaces on a marathon run.

More questions followed.

'I see your credentials in English as being a fair jump into our firm.' And the yellow marker came out again.

The next question actually took me by surprise.

'If we employ you, would you be willing to occasionally do a bit of debt collecting?'

I had some unfounded assumptions like, boxer, still in shape, am I to also be the private dick? I studied his unblinking eyes and hoped he would elaborate.

'I see an expression of concern, and I'm not surprised. I'm not looking for a bully boy, just a well set-up, well dressed man who could on occasions follow up on some debts which are overdue to us from agents, especially a man who can walk carefully in the night, I might say.'

'Yep. Not a problem, though I don't own a car.'

'That can be arranged. Are you in?'

'My bloody oath, Mr Banks.'

He stood up and I saw how tall he was.

He pushed out his hand and spoke. 'Can you start on Monday, Edgar – eight-thirty a.m. sharp?'

'I'm a punctuality freak, Mr Banks.' I thought I'd get that in straight away.

'I'm Les. Everyone calls me that. You'll be among mainly World War II vets who are great editors and you can learn a lot from them. I'll start you off on collections of short stories. See you on Monday.'

'Thank you, Mr – sorry, old habits – Les.'

*

I owed it to my parents to tell them the news, but I was not yet prepared to tell Dad about Bart and the big problems. It was still too raw and I might be able to catch him in a good mood when he might listen to me without any interruptions. He would have to be put in the picture of my good fortune obtaining a job with one of his old army mates.

Mum was different. I could always test the water with her before I had a problem about which to tell Dad.

She gave me a great hug. 'Marvellous, son. I'm vindicated as well because I always wanted to be an author and maybe I ought to start now. All those books I used to read to you have come home to roost. All of those phrases in your head. Blame me.'

'Okay, Mum, say one of them – just off the top of your head.'

She smirked and said, 'Righto, big shot. Here's one from the great Jane Austen.' And out it rolled as if she had read the book the night before: 'It is a truth universally acknowledged that a single man in possession of a good fortune must be in want of a wife.'

And I knew where my love for creative writing came from and in that moment my destiny was shaped. 'No wonder we all love you,' I chirped.

'Go and tell your dad before he finds out on the grapevine. Might settle him down about his sister, and the rapist who's back inside again – so much for his degree.'

5

My New Career

I began my new career of seventy per cent learning the craft of editing and thirty per cent as a bailiff, which involved more paperwork for accreditation. Aside from the debt stuff, we were also asked at times to liaise with other publishers. One of them comes into sharp focus when I recall what I had to do to achieve the best result.

I sat in a comfortable leather lounge inside the Old London Hotel waiting on the arrival of a high-profile publisher who was already twenty-five minutes late. My annoyance was growing, but I had to push it away as I did not wish to upset the man, much due to the money he was paying Les for my services. I kept glancing at my watch and told myself I would wait another half hour and then give it a miss. Mobile phones were not about back then. I had learnt one thing in the few months that I had worked as a subeditor, which was that it never pays to let the customer make all the rules. If he can push you around, he may assume other people can too, and that's not what he hires you for.

The old barman drifted past and glanced at the half Scotch and ice, which had by now melted. I shook my head and he moved away to another customer nearby.

I was still staring at my watch when a voice close to my elbow said, 'I'm shockingly late. I must apologise. You must forgive me. My name is Terrance Fallow. You're Edgar of course.'

I turned my head and looked at him. Middle-aged, rather plump, dressed as if he didn't give a thought about it; well shaved and with a thin crop of smoothed hair drooping onto a wide forehead.

He patted a bulging shabby old briefcase and yanked out some manuscripts. 'Three brand-new book-length scripts. It would be embarrassing to lose them before we have a chance to reject them.'

He clicked his fingers to the shuffling barman. 'Double Scotch on ice. Will you join me, Edgar?'

I couldn't wait – free drinks don't come round too much and it was a fair bet it would be single malt – so I just nodded and pretended to be nonchalant.

He soon got down to the business in hand, with a much more authoritative tone. 'One of our most important authors lives near here,' he said in a casual tone with the hint of an edge. 'Maybe you know him and his stuff – William Moore.'

'Can't say I do.'

He went on with his story, which would soon be my act one. 'I take your point. Historical romances, but they sell – brutally.'

I got in my fourpence-worth and replied, 'Now I know. I thought his stuff was tripe.'

'You're right but the point is that he's an automatic best-selling writer.'

There was a pause while we sipped our Scotch (which *was* single malt). I put down my empty glass and he clicked his fingers again.

'What do you want of me?'

He licked his lips and addressed the question. 'Moore is an alcoholic. He has lost the plot and he's going to pieces. He shot through for a week and it looks like he's in need of a shrink.'

It all begged another question from me. 'How do you know that you're going to reject them?'

'Righto. If they were any good, they would not be dropped off at my front door.'

'Then why take them on board anyway?'

'Partly not to hurt his feelings. However, there is a chance that all publishers live for. Sometimes at cocktail parties someone drops an unpublished script in your face. You ignore it but later it turns up on a secretary's desk and we have to go through the motions of reading it all – it's part of the job. I usually only read the first two chapters.'

I didn't get his point, as it seemed to lead nowhere. Maybe it was the double Scotches that he kept on ordering.

'Look, it may be a script that we might miss. But he needs a visit by you to set things straight. Not to leave scripts lying about which someone can steal and use. Get it?'

It fell into place.

He went on with the story. 'His wife doesn't agree that he's lost the plot. She's convinced that something is wrong and worrying him, like blackmail – maybe some jerk thinks that one of the stories which Moore wrote is really about him. There are some nutty people about. To nail it, we really want to know what ails him.'

'Tell me about it – the nuts, that is.'

'Maybe he has a guilty secret.'

And I know all about guilt.

'Give me the details and I'll go and have a chat to him – or maybe his wife first – and try to size him up. But my guess is she might just throw me out the house.'

He looked at me and smiled, showing a set of perfect white teeth. 'I have a feeling she's going to like you. She's a stunner. And to help with the counselling bit, he too is a navy veteran.'

'Maybe that's the problem. Leave it with me.'

He left me Moore's details.

I rang the number and quickly told his wife the précis and that I too was in the navy. She invited me to meet her at the house.

I was greeted by a tall red-haired woman who looked like Rhonda Fleming, one of my favourite actresses.

She called out loudly in a very husky Peggy Lee tone, 'William, Mr Williams is here.'

He came out of his study and we shook hands. I opened up and gabbled the message out as quickly as I could and all the time he stared at the top of my head, not my eyes. I pointed out the predicament and added a little bit about my sea time as well, which I believe broke the veiled look on his eyes.

I added, 'Anything you say is in the strictest of confidence. I know this as I was virtually pushed out of the navy for a minor infraction, though I told the commander to get fucked, which he really didn't appreciate.'

The ice was broken and I could see a chip coming off the sad face.

He stood up and stared at his wife, who remained seated and then put her hands over both ears. Like an old story which he once told but came back in spades to this time.

'I had an affair with a navy cook for a short time when I was young and stupid, silly me, I put it in a story which was published as fiction.'

'Phew,' I gasped. 'Can you tell me where he lives and his name?'

He went into his study and came out with a memo pad.

'Look, there has to be a compromise along the track.'

He sat forward, waiting.

'Change the name for a start, change his job in the navy and change the setting. Make it another country. If possible, save a free copy for him. But I wouldn't suggest you invite him to a launch. Has he asked for money?'

'No, he's rolling in it.'

'OK, if that's acceptable, give me his details and I'll catch up to him and give him a signed copy of the book.'

His wife took her well manicured hands off her face.

I called back the next day for the alterations. It did not take long. He looked like a man on a mission.

One week later, I met up with Oliver and his partner (also ex-navy) and we sat together. I told them my story about the vacuum cleaner and my demise and they laughed out loud.

'Come back, dear boy, and see us. No funny business, of course. We can have a few more laughs.'

Les slapped me on the back and said, 'I knew you could do it, Edgar. Thanks a million.'

There were not too many debt collector jobs coming after that as the company ended up using a firm of private detectives, whose services could be claimed against tax.

Les passed a lot more scripts to me and I was learning fast.

One of my favourite colleagues was Fred, who had a foot blown off in the Middle East. He gave me some good tips. I handed him a script from a woman who had written a historical novel. There was something about it that didn't gel with me.

Fred read it and knew instantly what was missing. 'The crux of the matter is one single incident which changed the world forever and she needs to put it in the first chapter.'

'Any suggestions, then?'

'The setting is India but Gandhi isn't mentioned, for some reason. When Gandhi was thrown off a train by a racist South African official in Durban, he closed his eyes and saw the British Empire crumbling. Across the world. That one episode changed the course of history.'

How prophetic those words were. It was a pivotal moment for me, the new boy on the block. I never forgot it. I wrote back to the author and she grabbed the advice with both hands. The book became a bestseller and it was all down to me asking for advice.

Around this time, I found my old baseball and glove, which I turned to for help with thinking when I was stuck. It helped me to solve the issues that editors are surrounded with.

*

My first marriage to a widow without any children went west and ended up in divorce. I didn't put all the blame on her of course, as it does take two to tango. However, I was on my own for a time and a nitpicking wife was not on my menu. She walked away without any regrets but I had some because no one in the family had ever divorced, a fact which Dad frequently reminded me about. And as well a marriage just can't rely on sex alone to keep it going smoothly. I had heard that she returned to her homeland in New Zealand. Funny, though, she now wrote short stories but had hated me spending time scratching away.

There were other life-changing events. The company closed down and all the great guys I worked for retired. Sadly, Les died soon after from a stroke and I went to his sad but celebrated funeral, which much of the publishing world attended to say goodbye.

I met many of them at the chapel afterwards. One older guy asked if I would like to buy his business in Geelong. I had a look at it and signed up. A secretary called Mary came with the package, and became my right arm, and I was now a publisher, with a hell of a lot of connections under my belt and not too far from the family home.

I was thirty-four years of age and I had some medals, which came in the post. The Australian Service Medal, the Korean Medal and the Malayan Campaign Medal. They hung in the front room of the office. Not bad for a bloke who was virtually forced out of the navy. At that point, I had still not told Dad why I left. There just had to be the right time to put it all together.

It was on my mind to get married again but due to the fact that I was busy, there did not seem the time to scout around; having kids was on my mind a lot. And then I met Jane in a whirlwind. At times, I look back and I wonder about stalking. In our case, who stalked who? She was more than presentable, with expensive gear, not a blonde hair out of place, which reminded me of Lana Turner. The perfect accent with just a wisp of a lisp delivered with words chosen between gaps. Yet no smiles followed on from the pauses.

There I was, sucked in by the prospect of a good life in which I could indulge myself with dreams of meeting famous New York writers.

There should have been a telegraph registering after she had met Mum. She fidgeted all through the half-hour, tapping her fingers on the kitchen table, and then at least five trips to the toilet, returning with a new shade of lipstick. Mum said nothing when Jane stood up, in a rush to the door. I ought to have listened and seen the signs but I was bent on marriage and kids before it was too late. And always in my mind was my past failure.

We were married in an unforgettable ceremony. I thought that my parents were wealthy but my in laws were loaded. He was a Supreme Court judge in Victoria and at times I thought that Jane had married out of her social level because she had gone to the best school, met the best of people and dined with servants at their elbows. I had my doubts once I knew how upper crust they were and whether I would fit it. I just had to plug along for the sake of peace. Try to be kind.

It didn't work. There was no gift that I could give her which would cement us. She was always off with her mother on shopping sprees. I was a virtual outcast until our twins were born. No shock there, as Dad was a twin. I jumped up a bit on their ladder when I tried really hard to cater for her every need.

But one thing really got my guts. They looked down on my beloved mum and I heard my mother-in-law once whisper to Jane, 'Just look at those goodbyes' (referring to Mum's upper-arm flab wobbling when they waved goodbye).

Then I spent more time in the office, hoping it would improve. It just got worse. The signs were there and a man would have to have been a mug to not see them. Jane wanted a front man and a father to her kids, if only to appease the gossipy women who fawned on her and laughed at her silly jokes. Most of them were about poorer people than them. I was like a store dummy in a window – trotted out, dressed up in the best digs and removed when better clothing and better dummies were found.

Jane was the indulged only child who could pick and choose at will. Maybe that picking was a man who wasn't too bad to look at and was also a publisher and an author. All of those attributes gave her bragging rights and those rights continued when in company, surrounded by a bevy of women, from young to ancient pretty to ugly, who all wanted their memoirs published. I was nudged quite a lot in that direction but resisted, which caused a bit of flak from Jane. I had made a rule earlier not to publish family or a friend, following advice given to me by my old friend Fred.

Sex started out fine on the honeymoon but it faded within months to almost nothing. Just some mechanical fumbles, which left neither party with any satisfaction. I was left with a thought – the vacuum cleaner; but I realised how much trouble that had caused in my life and allowed the thought to lie as part of my ego from a long time ago.

My comfort from a strange coupling was my kids Jillian and Joe, who were my lasting joy. I made sure that I rescued them from the clutches of my mother-in-law, Sarah, who incidentally, after a few years, had posted her husband, the judge, into the rumpus room, and of course his club, which also sent a signal to me: like mother, like daughter.

I wasn't wrong, as I found out when I attended a launch in Melbourne. I had to stay overnight in a five-star hotel as there was another launch the next day in Healesville, that well-wooded tree-studded town.

The alarm clock rang at eight a.m. and I jumped out of bed, shaved, showered, dressed and ate a piece of toast and marmalade (not as good as Mum's home-made variety).

I heard some laughter and voices of a man and woman outside my window. One of the voices sounded familiar. I peered out through the blinds. And there he stood in his pinstriped Italian suit with his Italian shoes and his old school tie and planting what looked like a tongue kiss on the younger woman's welcoming lips. They both had expensive satchels in their hands. She might have been his clerk – close to home.

I suppressed the rising laughter. The judge, the pillar of society and my father-in-law, was engaged in what appeared to be a hot love affair. A whisper came upon my lips of well, well, well, with another thought coming through that this was his escape from the rumpus room, and bloody good luck to him. Hypocrisy floated in the air but I knew all about that sin. All the money in the world had not brought their marriage contentment, and it wasn't hard to surmise that pompous Sarah knew all about it and accepted it.

Two vows were made right there. I would not let them rule my kids and if they tried I would blurt out what I saw on that day in the hotel. Last but not least, if Jane wanted to separate, I would not stand in her way, because if we stayed married I would have had a choice. The choice which Tim took: have an affair rather than be controlled by a sour-faced wife.

It all came to fruition just as I thought it would. At the age of forty, after six years of marriage, Jane took the kids to her parents' spacious home, with a swimming pool and a tennis court. Her father paid for the most expensive schools for my kids. I did not wish to stand in the way of a top education for the children but it caused me some sleepless nights about the level of indulgence, and whether it would change them.

The black nights had brought into my mind a feeling of failure. Was I a loser, which is not an expression I ever choose for anyone. Maybe I should have compromised. Would that have altered my soul? Yes, it would have. I had some therapy during that time and Mary's great support helped. She was a woman who still endured the sadness of watching her husband slowly drifting off with the dreaded MS. I valued her words.

I sank my words of regret into the delete box within my mind. But I could not get rid of Black Bart and the eventual satisfaction of how I stitched him up. Anyone who knew the story would think it was just pure vengeance and over the top. Who cares? I did it. I loved it and in spite of the subsequent scenes which came and eventually went, I have to say it was coming to Bart.

*

Black Bart's retirement was made known to me by a phone call to Mary one day. She did not know him and she said how arrogant he was on the phone and making demands. He had written his memoirs and would the firm be able to publish them? I waited with great hope and expectation of what I might say – or do – to him if he rocked up, and that was how it started.

6

The Clash

Did he know it was me he was dealing with? I doubted it, yet he was still arrogant and full of himself and might expect me to touch my forelock and stand straight. Or just let old wounds heal. Not bloody likely. If it was his forelock, I had a mind to sink a claw hammer into it. If it hadn't been for him, I might have retired with the rank he had.

I know that people might say – you were caught with a sex toy, so big deal, it would soon be forgotten. However, unless you have been in the navy you would not understand that something like that will blacken an officer for his entire career. The navy is judgemental and never forgets. If you're unlucky to be caught, you'll be assigned to the back paddock and treated like a leper.

Some what-ifs don't go away; they stick like dandruff on a black jumper. What if I had spent more time at home rather than frequently travelling interstate? That could apply to any job, I think. As to Black Bart, when he rang Mary and asked if we were accepting submissions, she quickly put him in the picture that we were running about fifty books behind. She told him to send a synopsis and the first chapter.

Bart was not satisfied and wanted to speak to the publisher. He was informed that I was away on business. He abruptly hung up the phone, as I had seen him do many times when he was on the bridge. Another spoiled brat, I was told by the guys, who actually hated him. He ignored her advice and dropped off the script on the front counter. It was very bulky and could have worked as a jumbo jet wheel chock.

About one hundred and twenty-five thousand words, which usually would cause any publisher to groan, 'Oh no.'

Mary rang him and spoke about his careless regard for the rules of the office regarding unpublished scripts. That was what I loved about her. Her no-nonsense approach.

'Mr Smith –'

He corrected her with his full name but she kept on.

'Mr Smith, this is not what I told you to do when we spoke on the phone, remember?'

He started to shout at her again. 'I am a decorated senior naval officer and I expect a bit more respect from you. I don't care about your stupid rules. My name in full is J. Bartholomew-Smith. Do you hear me?'

'Follow the rules, Mr Smith. Nothing will change. It will probably not be read. If you don't like it, send it to another publisher.'

'Where is your manager?'

'I haven't got one.'

'I will report you.'

'Go for it, dickhead.' She slammed down the phone.

He was back at the office within two hours, so I guessed he lived nearby. He thumped the desk and she knew who he was.

'See that exit sign. Just turn round and leave.'

He obeyed someone, for once in his life, and made an about turn. In the process, he tripped on the front mat and sprawled on the floor.

Mary bent over to help him up but he brushed her hand away and yelled out, 'You will hear more from me very soon.' He left the office, leaving his script on the desk.

She heard him revving his car loud. Smoke came out of the exhaust. She saw him laughing but his laugh soon stopped when a local speed cop stepped off his bike and looked at the exhaust. She saw the cop writing out a defect notice, which was placed on the windscreen of the car.

Bart was in a rage and waved his finger in the cop's face.

The cop promptly twisted the finger back, and said quite loudly, 'Have a good day, Mr Smith.'

'I've got your number. I am a retired naval officer.'

'That's good. Did you sail on *Popeye*?'

'My name is Bartholomew-Smith. Is everyone stupid in this street?'

The cop pressed his starter button and rode off.

'I couldn't stop laughing,' said Mary afterwards, when she told me on the phone what had transpired.

I roared at the part about the cop asking, 'Did you sail on *Popeye*?' because Bartholomew-Smith did have pop eyes.

'I can't wait, Edgar, to hear what you'll do with the script.'

'Trust me, Mary, I have a few scores to settle with him, let me reassure you.' I had a plan.

*

I was at work at seven a.m. and started to read the first two chapters of Bart's book. After many passages of absolute narcissism, bordering on psychotic comments, I had enough. It was drivel and not worthy of publishing, though some would say I was biased.

Mary was working shorter hours due to her husband's ill health and I was on my own with my thoughts.

I went into the toilet area and dropped the script on a stool. I dropped my trousers and when I was ready, after looking at a dirty book, I started to masturbate and ejaculated over the first two pages of the book. I waited till it was dry, which took a long time. I closed the book and put it back in the bag which it came in. I placed the usual rejection slip inside the parcel, with the words 'This manuscript is not suitable for this business. I wish you well.' I didn't but that is what is usually written.

A week later, he burst through the front door like a September shower and announced in his usual manner, 'Where is the manuscript?'

Mary buzzed me but I stalled. I'm sure he did not recognise me when I slowly walked out. He marched forward with his right hand stretched out but I stepped aside and as a result he shook hands with the desk calendar instead.

He spun round in anger and called out, 'What sort of show is this?'

It was my time to speak after all those years on the ship. 'You don't remember me, do you?'

'I can't say I do.'

'Remember back in 1955 on the *Sydney* when you humiliated me?'

His eyes veiled over and then he clicked his fingers. 'Hoover. It's Hoover.'

'That's what you named me in front of a lot of sailors.'

His eyes flicked away from my gaze for a second while he looked at the top of my head. 'Shit, that's a hell of a long time ago.'

'Do you remember, after all that was said to me, that you demanded an answer from me?'

He looked blank.

'I'll refresh your memory. I said, "Get fucked, sir."'

A look of recognition flashed into his bloodshot eyes. 'Yes, I do remember. I gave you two weeks in the brig for insolence.'

'That ruined the career that was mine for the taking.'

He took time to absorb my remarks and got off the track from 1955, trying to divert me.

'Your manuscript is absolute crap. We are not going to publish it.'

His eyes bulged and his face went red. Mary had just arrived back, as her husband was all right, and the doctor was at the house. She handed him the manuscript parcel and he fled out the door. I watched from the window as he unwrapped it, and the mushroom smell must have hit his nostrils.

He rushed inside again, with his fists raised towards me, his mouth open with the protruding teeth snapping his words, 'You've blown your bolt all over the book.'

I stepped closer and said with a smile, 'Only the first two pages really.'

He took a swing at me, but it went wide. He must have forgotten that I was a boxing champion on the ship. I blocked it, stepped in and gave him the old one-two, midriff and the side of his head. But they were soft punches and did not draw blood. It was not my intention to really hurt him badly.

He lay on the floor moaning. Mary helped him up and put him in his car. He sat for a few minutes and then drove off.

Within a few hours, two cops arrived on the doorstep. I gave them a quick précis but they didn't seem to believe it till Mary stepped in.

'Excuse me. It was self-defence. I saw the lot. He came at Edgar with his fists raised, all because we wouldn't publish his book. I can make a statement to that effect.'

The cops looked at one another and nodded. One started taking a statement from Mary.

'He claims that you did a blow job on his manuscript.' He looked at me with a smile forming.

'He'll have to prove it. The book wasn't used as a weapon.'

'Would you consent to a test?'

'You'll have to get permission from my lawyer. Don't like your chances, though.' I thought then it was not a time to come out as a smart arse.

The older cop told me he would report it and I would receive a summons.

I attended court within a few days with my lawyer John, who knew the magistrate. They went into the chambers with the prosecutor.

Thirty minutes later, John walked out with a grin on his face. He had told the magistrate the whole story about my indiscretion (if you could call it that). The magistrate replied that he would set a date for a directions hearing as the matter appeared to be a civil one.

I attended but the annoyed man didn't and the case was thrown out for lack of any real evidence. It's not an offence to ejaculate on a book. But a civil claim might be allowed for damages.

*

Three months later, I read the death notices and apparently Bart had died of dementia in a nursing home. There were all sorts of accolades plastered in the notices. Someone must have loved him. End of story.

Mary had to know the full story because her lips pursed at times about the desecration of the manuscript.

'Get a glass of that great Hunter white and take the phone off the hook.'

She brought out the wine and two glasses with ice. And sat waiting for me to open up with the story from go to whoa. And I went off, from the vacuum cleaner, to the steward, to the bridge, to the humiliation, to my reply of 'Get fucked, sir' and the consequences.

She sat back absorbing the lot. She was a woman of the world. And I knew she would have some questions.

'So you used a sex tool for relief – so what, they're everywhere now. Beats masturbation, I suppose. It has been said that with masturbation one gets to meet a better class of person.' She shrieked and I joined in.

'So you kept the vacuum cleaner, then?'

'Yep. I was going to chuck it on his grave but I thought about karma.'

'Wise move. What happened after they let you out of the brig?'

'The dickhead had me scrubbing his cabin floor. I spotted his old group school photo. It was Geelong Grammar, where my dad went. Dad the class captain was in the front and the dickhead was at the back. I'm yet to talk to Dad about it. Something must have happened between them for me to be the whipping boy payback man.'

'Let me know, pull-lease. What about the slimy steward who couldn't wait to put you down?

'You never know, there may be closure on that one as well. Actually, I spotted him one night outside the RSL, in Geelong, do you mind? I might just go there one night and let him know who I am.'

*

Fortune must follow the brave because not long after our little talk I spotted the weasel outside the RSL, piddling on a bush. He turned round. I saw how frail he was. I thought to hit him but that would not erase my thoughts about him.

'Do you remember me?' I said as he was doing up his zipper.

'Should I?' he slurred.

'Hoover. Does that ring a bell?'

'Bloody hell.'

I left him with his thoughts and walked away.

7

Celebrities

I've published the memoirs of many celebrities. From rock stars, sports people, actors and even some writers. Most of them who I met were nonchalant and were pushed into autobios by agents who had their eyes fixed on the royalties. Some of the stars' life stories were questionable and veracity was always a problem. How many toes would they step on? And as publishers there was always a risk for us as well. Like copyright and angry families threatening to sue. It was not a bag of goodies, so why did we do it? If we all gave up, our generations would be bereft of good books. Does that make me a crusader? I think not but I prefer to believe I'm giving back something good for the world.

The celebrities made a lot of money from books about themselves and that was what it all boiled down to, in spite of airy-fairy people saying how wonderful it is to put words on paper so that some people might read. How wonderful it is for books to be on shelves. But the cost of printing makes books an expensive exercise. Libraries regularly put out good books after a short time at a cheap price. The only book I can think of which has transcended the centuries is the Bible, which has had many fingers involved in altering God's word, as my dad said.

Johnny Bean was, however, my most memorable celebrity. He had heaps of regrets straight after the book I did for him went viral right around the world. Johnny, the leader of a well known rock band, chose to exploit all of his sexual antics, fights with band members, his ex-wives and even his siblings. His book drew enemies. Some held up placards with words such as 'You're going to hell J.B.'

Johnny banged on my office door one cold night in spite of the closed sign. I guessed he had heard me tapping away.

'You've got to help me, Edgar,' he blurted out. 'Let me stay here just for the night, mate. You're the only one I can trust. Everybody else is out to kill me.' He cleared his throat and spat into a tissue. 'I was followed by a jerk who tried to run me off the road.'

He glanced furtively over his shoulder at the front door; he closed the venetian blinds, all the time with his back to the wall and out of view to anyone who might be standing on the street. After that, his face muscles relaxed but I saw his hand shaking as he put it in his pocket.

He was twenty-nine but on that night he looked older. His mottled face and sunken eyes betrayed a desperate, fearful man. The Roman nose showed a sign of acne, spreading from the tip to the bridge. His high cheekbones and wet lips, which he was licking in a circular motion, were a sight which had never reached the tabloid magazines.

He wore a black leather jacket, tailored jeans, pointed-toe black boots, and a bright blue shirt open to his solar plexus. Dangling chains of twenty-two-carat gold draped down from his open collar to the last button on his shirt.

I finally spoke. 'I see.' The two words were delivered as calmly as I could in that moment. 'So everybody is trying to kill you.'

He fingered his gold chains as if it was a precursor to an inner mantra.

I peered out the window and then spotted a full moon, which, in conjunction with a little too much cocaine and his weekly visits to some sort of spook, had sent him over the top, which was not surprising for a guy who was already a trifle paranoid.

I came up with an initial solution. 'Let's call Suzie,' I said, 'and see if she'll come and pick you up.'

'She left me. She hates me.'

I was now struggling with what to do with him. 'There must be someone…'

'You don't have anybody when you're where I am – old friends turn on you, they envy you. The success, the money. And then there are the agents, the lawyers who are jackals: they tie you up for years. I've become a slave for the rest of my life. It's a lot of shit, I'm telling you, Ed.' He rubbed his chains again and then pulled at them as if they were choking him. 'That's why I came here – I knew I could count on you.'

I interrupted him before he went too far into self-pity. 'Right, I'll tell you something else. I remember when you became a TV star. I also recall when you never returned my calls.'

'I was too busy,' he pleaded. He stared into my eyes and I opened up again.

I had to tell him that he was sliding. 'Get a life. No one is trying to kill you. Get off that bloody cocaine. It's blowing your ego up like a helium balloon. Get a grip before you end up as a street junkie.' I could see some tears forming in the corner of his eyes. What I said might have been a bit too blunt at this point in his life. I was not a shrink.

His voice lowered into a whisper. 'You're not going to help me then?' He started to turn towards the door.

I felt a bit of sorrow right then and I had to make an offer, even if it was half-hearted. 'If you really want to stay here...' I began.

He shrugged and with a half-smile said, 'What's the difference?' He had a self-deprecating tone with an edge of bitterness. 'Then it's all in my head, as you say. Too much fun, too much coke and too much fame, right, buddy?'

I did not know how to respond, because I had already said too much.

He patted my cheek with icy cold fingers and left through the door without slamming it. I was fearful for him, and it would not be too far from the truth to say that he was in a big pickle.

Two days later, his charred body was found in a burnt-out Mustang at the bottom of a cliff on the Great Ocean Road.

A traffic cop spoke on the television news that night. 'There are some suspicious circumstances.'

It left me with another what-if. Was I chalking up too many regrets?

8

Functions

Cocktail parties were a part of the publishing scene once. Most agents, critics, editors and that inevitable bunch of aspiring writers who were willing to pay good money, just to mingle in the hope of success. They were usually fixed on the great Australian novel in order to make a lot of money, maybe a movie, and settle back on an island.

It was all illusions for most of the pen-pushers. There are not too many Colleen McCullochs left in this country. There are a few who tap away with the mainstream publishers breathing down their necks. Yet once in a while a writer bobs up with something new and fresh. We start to track their progress from the one good book; however, the next version is pale in comparison

The looks of despair used to worry me once. They didn't any more. My armour had become impenetrable.

The last party (hopefully) that I went to only consolidated my view that nothing had changed. The same name-droppers of mixed and odd genders, cross-dressers and others, who looked like Gothic vampires, bounded around the room like unregistered dogs. During their sober moments, the topics such as wars, immigration and climate change (which was not really cared about at that time by the general public), were exchanged with some propriety, until the grog came out. As did the true natures.

I was between girlfriends on that New Year's Eve when I made a vow: never again. I didn't need the coke, the speed and spiked drinks to get high. I just longed to make a quick escape once the mascara started to run and the sloppy kisses started. My escape route was blocked by a drunken middle-aged woman who offered me all the sexual delights if I read her book. A trans-sexual person offered to pay me if I would shit on a glass table while he wanked underneath. The party was getting out of hand, and with the open patio doors on the high rise, it was not beyond imagination that someone would fall from that great height.

I made my way down to the ground floor and stood outside smelling the fresh air.

'Hi,' said the petite woman about thirty-eight smoking a cigarette. 'You don't know me. I went to a book launch at Healesville some time ago when you were selling the books for my friend.'

I remembered that the books had sold very well. 'Jenny.'

She nodded. And added a bit about her life. I listened.

'I'm a children's book illustrator. Sold a few. Oh, I'm Jackie,' and she stuck out her tiny hand, which I shook.

After that, she was silent and seemed to withdraw into herself. I wasn't into kids' books then, but openings were punctuating the atmosphere in those micro-seconds. I looked at her left hand: there were no rings or white marks. She looked good but I slowed down and just gave her my card. She produced her card. I waved goodbye and caught a taxi home. She was on my mind but I decided to let the universe work it out.

The depression I had about not seeing my kids for some time faded when I brushed my teeth before hitting the sack. It was one of those nights when the air is heavy and the night noises seem muffled and far away. There was a high misty moon. I got up and played a few records. Nat King Cole was singing, 'Be happy when you're blue, it isn't very hard to do and you'll find happiness without an end whenever you pretend.' It was appropriate for me.

I dozed and heard a ticking somewhere but there wasn't anything in the house that ticked. The ticking was in my head. It was like I was on a death watch. Change was coming.

It was daylight when I finally dropped off and dreamed all the time of protagonists and a pile of unpublished scripts, and the tricks which could be used by writers to create a hook to suck in the buyer. They darted about in my head and the genre of suspense was prominent in my visual images image of a murderer.

The murderer in fiction is always the one you guess is the killer. There are people who kill out of hate, or fear or greed. There are cunning killers who are just in love with death to whom murder is a remote kind of suicide. In a sense, they are all insane, but not in the fashion which comes from the pen of the writers who are cool in the genre of suspense.

My mind has to learn to put all of those scary scripts into boxes so that I can let them sit until I find a writer who has a voice and who is inside of the skin of the created characters.

It isn't that easy. Writing, editing and publishing must be the hardest art of all.

9

Father and Son

Nothing much was spoken by Dad about my exit from the navy. I hoped the subject might come up because I yearned to unload the whole damn lot, irrespective of whether I got a form of judgement lecture about sticking my nose to the grindstone and coping with troubles along the way. I had heard it all before.

But I was wrong.

It was after one of Mum's great Sunday roasts, when he and I sat outside just absorbing the sun beaming down on us on a great November day. I was happy because my kids were there as well, and Mum was in her element, fussing around them.

He lit his pipe while we sat side by side on the swinging hammock with the shade on top. It was not an adversarial situation, unlike the times I remembered when we used to chat with him opposite, on a higher chair.

I opened the long-awaited dialogue. 'Did you know I found out that Bart and you were at school together?' (I had already sent him a card before Bart started out on me, and his return notice to me then was neither positive nor negative. I guess he was waiting for something, to be inclined to the negative.)

He swung round on the chair, shifting his position. He had a surprised look on his face. He banged his pipe on the side of the chair. His voice was calm when he spoke. 'Tell me how you knew, son.'

I told him how I was treated like a servant and had to scrub Bart's cabin floor. 'Then I saw the school photo where you were in the front and he was squeezed at the back.'

'I forgot about that photo, son. So you guessed that's where the bad blood came from. Do go on.'

I went into a narrative of what had happened with the vacuum cleaner and the steward who couldn't wait to dob me in. I paused and verbalised what my thoughts had been back in those moments. 'Before that, I thought we might have been enemies in a past life, because the air was so toxic that it was tangible. You could cut the air with a knife from the time we met. The name must have touched a nerve.'

Dad looked down and seemed to be speaking to the freshly mown grass under our feet. Then he spoke. 'I'll tell you my story, and then you can tell me yours, OK?'

I couldn't wait to hear what happened between him and Bart.

'He boarded all the time at school, though he came from a family with a lot of wealth. I don't know what happened at his home – it was a bit of a mystery. Some of the lads reckoned he bullied his younger siblings, and that proved to be right soon enough. Leopards don't change their spots. He was a bully, that I know. They were smaller kids. He wouldn't have tried that on some of my mates. They would have knocked him into next week.'

I was transfixed.

Dad topped up his pipe and then went on. 'He was also a hypocrite. And I tagged him as a coward. However, he was on the *Australia* in the Battle of the Coral Sea and any cowardice would have had him put on the next passing cargo ship home, and out of the navy, so I give that to him.'

Dad took a long swig on his Carlton draught beer and restarted the story. 'I was at the block urinal after a game of football and near the bushland at the back. I heard someone sobbing. I stood on tiptoe and looked through the window bars. And there was Bart up against a tree with his trousers down. He was being sucked off by the smallest kid in the school – young Jamie – but to my eternal damnation, which still haunts me, I said nothing. I should have, because poor Jamie jumped in front of a train two days later.'

I just sat there, gulping back saliva. I realised my faultless father had inner turmoils to deal with, just like me. I recovered and interjected while Dad was catching his breath. Hypocrisy stood out in bold like a great immovable rock in a waterfall. Dad was still sucking in the emotion and tears welled up in his eyes.

'Bloody hypocrite' was all I could add but I knew there had to be more than just what Dad had seen in the urinal.

'When we heard about poor Jamie, some of the kids looked shamefaced because they had bullied him with words. "Guess what," Bart says, and we all leant forward. "He was a bloody homo anyway." I couldn't pull my punch. It flattened him to the ground and he was out for a time. We just left him there with his bloodied face. I never said why I did it, but I reckon he knew and maybe it haunted him. Funny about people like that. They all try to push the blame on others. Like Doreen would say. Just like King David. Just like Henry VIII. Always someone else's fault.'

A long silence followed this time until he prompted me. I filled him in with the vacuum cleaner and up to the humiliation.

Dad listened and spoke carefully. 'What was your reply to him after all the bullshit?'

'Get fucked, sir.'

A great grin came on his face which widened into a bellowing laugh. He held his stomach until it stopped. I was laughing with him in cadence as well. I had never seen such mirth coming from him when I was a kid, and as an adult I enjoyed it.

It slowed down and I asked the question, 'What about the vacuum?'

He astonished me with his man of the world response. 'Just a bloody sex toy. Who cares? What's the difference between a hand and a toy? It's what men do. Trust me, when I was away I saw a hell of a lot of the five-finger shuffle, or feeding the chooks, or spanking the monkey. Just an outlet and nobody suffers – unless you fall in love with the object. I'm glad you didn't marry the vacuum cleaner. Because it would have been another bad marriage.'

'You just had to get that in, Dad. Didn't you?'

'I have a feeling that Bart hasn't yet gone off the radar for you, son.'

I didn't have the heart to tell him the scenario of Bart's manuscript. I would save it for later when I got him on my own again, which was not too often those days.

*

It was shock time within a few days of the roast dinner. Dad had a lot to tell me and he came to the office. I made him a cup of coffee and his face was quite pale.

His words tumbled straight out, which was unusual for him, as he was used to delivering words in a carefully structured style. 'Doreen has breast cancer. Surgery won't cure it. She wanted me to tell you. Joan knows, because she's overseas with Jack. I took a drink and it didn't help. I muttered words like how, when, why, but it was to no avail and I couldn't put the words together.'

He knew I had a question – what son wouldn't have?

He answered, 'Maybe three to six months.' And then the tears came with the sobs.

Mary rushed in and held his shoulder. It didn't help.

'She doesn't want to see anyone at the moment. She's in hospital.'

I beckoned to Mary. 'Can you stay? I'll take him home.'

She nodded vigorously.

We went outside.

'Can you take me to the club? I want to tell the boys.'

'Of course, Dad.'

I took him to the club and he told me to go home; the boys would bring him back. I obeyed and went back to the office. I stayed awake and a call came. I jumped to the phone. It was Dad: could I come over? It wasn't far, so I drove, carefully. The porch light was on and Dad came to the door.

'Come in, son. I have something to tell you – no, it isn't Mum.'

I sat down.

He started to talk. 'Look, when we're gone, look through the papers. We're very well-off – I always brought properties. Shares are too risky. Mum might survive this. She has a strong heart. I've already bought a residential village place with all that opens and shuts. We can get a carer in as well and if either of us gets bad there's a hospice in the centre. I'm giving the house to you and I suggest you use the big double garage at the front as an office. Joan's getting some properties as well. You're a bit too young to retire so I guess you'll still publish. There are units for the two kids and other monies in the bank. You don't need to make a decision yet but of course if it goes bad I would like you to stay in the house. Have you taken all that in?'

My concerns were only fixed on Mum and hope. But it was a generous offer which I could not refuse. 'Of course, Dad. I'll make arrangements to move in very soon.'

He leaned over and hugged me, which was a milestone for me.

We visited Mum nearly every day and, though it was sad to see her with all of the tubes and so on, we managed a laugh. My two kids held her hands all the time. She survived past the six months and by then Dad had moved to the village and a new life waited for her.

And a new one for me as well, with many changes. I was living at the old house and I still had the office in town and was not sure if I should move the office – after all, it was Dad's suggestion – but I had Mary, my loyal mate, to think about as well. I knew that she was in bit of a pickle with a mortgage over her head and I came up with something which I would talk to her about. As I didn't need my unit any more, I wanted her to live in it, rent-free – I was not one to be too stuck on money. Dad had certainly fixed that with his careful purchases over the years so I would drive to work earlier than usual and talk to Mary about my suggestion. She was a proud person but not having to pay rent would be a blessing to her and poor Alf.

The alarm went off as usual and I went off as usual on my journey to the office.

10

The Hoodie

I locked the car and walked in the rain with an umbrella, not thinking about work. My mind fixed on the offer I would make to Mary. The black clouds and thunder, which always preceded anything which had been alarming to me in my life, ought to have been a warning sign of what lay beneath the shadows.

My mind was also fixed on my coming birthday; I would be forty-seven and I wondered where the time had gone. The X-ray after a funny cough was bad news for me because it showed a particle of asbestos in my lungs which was tracked right down to the source in 1955, on the *Sydney*, which had been awash with the dangerous stuff, floating everywhere.

The wonders of modern medicine astounded me. With some treatment, I'd be able to live till I was around seventy, but then it would be curtains. I spoke to a veterans' organisation about it and some medicine would be free but in light of Dad's wealth it would not be needed.

It bucketed down when I was close to the front door. I had my old golf club under my arm and the umbrella had gone haywire. I reached the door and suddenly felt a rumble in my stomach. Something was up – the door was ajar and that was not like Mary, who was very security-minded. I shook the drops off the umbrella and peered through the letter box opening.

I was confronted by the sight of Mary, crouched in a corner, holding a bleeding forearm up in the air, as was shown in her first aid course. I knew we had an intruder. I put down the umbrella and with one mighty shove I hurtled through the door. There he was, holding a great butcher's knife and wearing one of those nightmarish hooded jumpers. He jumped up and came towards me, threatening with the knife pointed out. I acted immediately, belting him right across the head with the golf club, then gave him another one just for good measure. He was out to it where he lay, spilling blood from his ears onto the new carpet. I kept my eye on him and rang for an ambulance.

The police arrived within a short time. The crook was still out to it.

The senior constable spoke first, staring at the prone man while the ambulance bandaged his head. 'It's Donald James – finally got caught.' He looked and me and the golf club I still held. 'Looks like self-defence to me. He copped a fractured skull.'

The younger cop was a bit brash and remarked, 'And he's permanently rehabilitated as well.'

I was concerned about Mary. 'Excuse me, guys. I have to get Mary to the hospital. She's lost some blood.'

'We'll take her for you. Good job, Mr Williams.'

I yelled out as they left, 'I'm getting too old for this shit.'

The silly bugger with the hood was still in a coma and if he came out they had a string of other robberies to ask him about.

*

Mary hugged me to bits when I told her about my plan for her. Her struggles had taken away any suggestion of no, not interested. I arranged a move for her to my three-bedroom unit and asked her if she wanted to keep the furniture. She immediately said yes. She deserved it for all her loyalty to me, and her poor husband.

11

Sadness

Dad was a giant figure in my life. I tried to model myself on him but it didn't work. We have to live with our own flaws and find a way to either quash them like a bug or use them to our advantage. I thought he was flawless, right up to the time about Jamie, and his silence about the wounds inflicted on the lad. How it stuck to Dad like an acorn, which grew over time into an oak. Yet it was the way of the world back then in Australia. Dobbing was not popular, but neither was cowardice. Men used their fists to deal with problems, as did the cops, who are really just an extension of civilisation. We get the cops we deserve and they get the people they deserve.

I had no issue with the law and I wondered where we would be without it. Chaos, I imagined, or would it be just like Soylent Green, where at age fifty we're given a drug, we slide down an elevator and come out the other side as biscuits, to feed a starving population.

I pondered on the new navy with many women on board. I had heard about sexual abuse. It still happened, although people like Bart would not last too long and would be replaced before mutiny reared its head.

I wondered about an afterlife. Was there a special place for people like my parents? I hoped so.

Dad had no right to die suddenly, even though he was approaching eighty years, but he missed his beloved Doreen, as we all did. They had a life which was not trumped and they died almost at the same time, Mum first and Dad not much later. It was a bugger, though, burying two parents in succession. I never had a chance to tell him about the final clash with Bart, which I was sure he would have approved. That is regret.

Their funerals were a celebration of their lives. It was a pity Jane was absent, though I guessed that was fair, because I never went to her parents' services after they were killed in a horrendous car crash with a B-double in the north. Not much was left of them, so they say. So much for bulk money. We all end up as chopped liver.

*

In spite of my great loss, I met up with Jackie, the kids' book artist. We dated, went to each other's launches and she became another rock for me, though she reckoned I was getting a bit grumpy. We lived together for some time and decided to take a chance on marriage. I had previous convictions for marriages and that was why I avoided the process for a fair period.

Jackie had a husband who blew out the door like a north wind after she refused to cover his gambling debts; the debts were owed to bikies. He was found face down in a park, with a plastic bag tied around his neck. Tied with a reef knot, which was loved by boy scouts. Was it one of those august troops? Who knew? Anyone is capable of murder, even boy scouts, doctors, parsons and priests; in times past, priests were skilled in the art of killing. All in the name of God. No wonder Mum was an atheist. Dad wasn't, though. A spell in a trench with artillery whistling overhead might make you think about God.

Jackie loved the old house and so did her kids when they visited. Yet I felt a growing anger when I moved towards sixty about kids starving in this wealthy country. Maybe I would retire and become an activist, because I was well on the way in the apprenticeship.

I'm asked about my take on happiness. Most of us get harmony and or contentment. We get over our wounds in time, though some wounds still stick to their guns, like little pinpricks. Perhaps it's a mental state, cured by fake it and you'll make it.

12

A Publisher's Thoughts About Writing

I loathe speaking to writers' groups, because of forceful authors trying to push unpublished scripts on me, unless they've read the website and considered the rules required for submission. But I kept copies of some of my speeches over the years to vast crowds of interested aspirants. This one is my favourite.

When it comes to writing, as in many things, you either do or you don't. It doesn't matter if your life is going right or wrong or whether you have the right kind of support or not. You own the pen and you choose to use it or not.

Everywhere you turn, you hear bad news about publishing houses. You hear about mainstream publishers closing their doors. Newspapers are folding and it seems that the only authors getting published are the few celebrities, or well known writers. The little guy doesn't stand a chance.

Before you hit the 'stuff it all' key, take a stroll through a bookshop and see the rows of print books. Writers filled those pages – men and women bent over their keyboards wrote, deleted, groaned, swore, ground on and banged their head, just the way you. They worked hard at writing the words and found a small publisher or a short story competition.

The most important rule on writing is 'Write to communicate, not to impress with fancy words no one uses nowadays.' It's better to be simple. The US writer Alice Walker describes her mother as a woman with a look which could make you sit down, all ears. Eleven simple words. Not only does she show the mother, you hear her say, 'Yes, mother.' Now that's a voice.

Today the reader who has no special interest in literature and reads for enjoyment usually finds discomfort in novels that use mainly narrative summaries to resonate what is happening offstage, and out of the reader's sight, hearing events told about, rather than witnessed.

It's important to understand the reason for a reader's discomfort. There has been a drastic change in storytelling in the twentieth century and the reason for that change is, unfortunately, not taught in school.

Writers need to know that we have all had exposure to movies, a visual medium, and for a half of a century a massive exposure to television, also a visual medium. Today's readers have learned to see strong happenings before their eyes. They tend also to skim or skip great slabs of narrative summary.

If you're looking to be published in today's world, there's no point in writing for dead audiences. You have got to get savvy and get into the century.

Animals rely most on their acute ability to smell or hear. Their vision is poor compared to humans. Vision is mankind's most important sense. Our interest in visual detail is a response to the most acute sense we have. It's called immediate scenes. If a scene isn't filmable, it isn't immediate.

As to fiction, the best novels don't give a laundry list of clothes worn by a character, or a paragraph of descriptions for a setting. The writer must employ particularity, choosing which significant detail characterises best. The reader is perfectly capable of filling in the rest. You need to depict an ill-fitting jacket, not the whole suit. You need a character's eye that looks everywhere at the speaker, but not the whole face.

That's just a peek at what is of interest to the publisher.

If you're starting out, then think about a collection of related stories. Peter Carey did it once and it hit the publishing world with a bang. Try novellas between around eighteen and twenty-three thousand words. If you're intent on something larger, check first on the net.

I hope this helps you as aspiring writers.

I received my first great ovation. A few questions came along and it was obvious that the audience were searching for something of value to assist in their journey.

A middle-aged woman stood up. 'Did you start off with something special which launched you into the writer's world?'

It was a good question and I started off slowly. 'I hung onto to a short poem which I didn't think would make it. It was a bit rude and was about my time in the navy.'

The audience straightened their backs and leaned forward, as if on a cue, like a marshall had told them to sit up straight.

'Yet in spite of that success, which put me on the map, there came a time when it was embarrassing, like dragging a trail of toilet paper around you on the bottom of your shoe.'

The audience chuckled.

'I was a bit like Captain Ahab, unrelenting, driving his crew, pursuing my personal Moby Dick despite possible disaster ahead, infecting his crew with a frenzy. I became obsessed with scribbling endless scripts. The crew of course was that inner man inside me. My muse, if you like. And most writers have an unknown friend.' I paused, took a breath and went on.' It was like sitting on top of a polar ice cap, just as global warming kicks in. I felt like a forgotten ghost ship lost in some fog when the rejections thundered in.'

A young woman with a shawl draped around her shoulders spoke in an arrogant tone. 'I didn't come here to get a lecture about some dopey other world.' She sat down.

I smiled. 'It's a free country and you're quite free to leave.'

Which she did. Hoots of laughter followed her out the door, which became stuck.

I yelled out, 'Hang on. Let's all pray for the door to open.'

The audience went silent and then the door swung open and, just as she was walking out, her shawl caught on the edge of the door. She tugged at it but it remained fast.

'Someone help her out before she gets it tangled around her throat and she strangles just like Isadora Duncan.' (Duncan was a celebrity whose shawl got caught in the wheels of her expensive sport's car.)

I guessed the cranky woman would never have forgotten the speech.

The episode inspired me to pronounce some more takes on life.

Each of us is like a boat passing through a long series of locks that lifts us up or takes us down to a new level. We go from one phase to another. Each change is a challenge: adulthood, marriage, divorce at times, getting old, changing jobs and becoming a parent. We're like a person in therapy who asks, 'Why do I keep coming back time after time and we sit and wait like a Chinese jar, implacable, never in motion? No change.'

Permeating and dominating our lives is the whole scene of intellectual sleepiness, encouraged by passive media such as movies, magazines and, God save me, reality TV, all of which offer no challenges to our intellect. Yet it can be challenged.

The way forward for writers is in one word: irony. See the irony in most issues. I don't expect you to be inoculating the masses, just look in your plots for irony and hypocrisy. It has been with a us a long time. As a general rule to get through life, develop a keen appreciation of those two words, for they're all around you. A little bit of clean honest wit can save you from heavy seriousness that gives lives a tragic tone. Life need not always be tragic. You can see through it and beyond. There's no need to be moralistic towards yourselves and others or become a victim to someone else's moralising attitude. Moralistic judgements are always based on anxiety. They sound high and righteous, but they come from a small, worried and badly concluded despair. Remember this and the truth will always flow out in the pages of your books. Readers are not stupid. Do not treat them in that fashion.

The audience stood up and cheered.

I spoke to a few ladies afterwards. One of the group asked me about envy.

'Be careful of it. If you're at the bottom of the writer's ladder, do not try to push the one in front out of the way. Think about it. Just quietly swing over to the other side of the ladder and make your way up, even reaching through and giving the other writer a hand.'

The crowd appeared to be pleased. Indeed, some might have been stunned.

13

In Closing

My son is a botanist after having obtained his degree. He had been going down that path since he was kid; he was always smelling flowers and breaking off leaves. In spite of my fears of indulgence, it never came to that. Kids really do make their own way in the world. He has moved into the science of propagating, which keeps him busy. His partner Lisa is a naval officer. (What about that for a turn around?) He reckons it's like a honeymoon every time Lisa's ship berths. Or they fly to some exotic location. I put my stepkids through an editor's course and I have given them part-time work as readers, although Jim loves his bricklaying job. Karen has a lot of art skills and she currently lives in Sydney with a musician in a country and western band.

I am at times a bit grumpier than usual but in spite of Jackie's comments (and she is a great exaggerator) I don't think they're frightened of me. Though I can bark at times and shout out about my favourite hate subjects – when I look at stupid reality TV, for example. Anyone hearing me would say, 'Yes, he is a grump.' I may have to control my outbursts as I'm told they can lead to the big D… dementia. Wasn't in my family or my ex-wives. Still, the asbestos hasn't gone away and I fear for another bout of blood on the tissue.

*

I've been a writer one way or the other all my life, thanks to Mum and her teachings. I am a publisher of other people's books as well, which has given me a bit of dough and a lot of long hours, plus an estrangement from the mother of my children on occasions. I was a would-be peacemaker when I started out in the trade and it seemed that I was like a United Nations emissary trying to get the Jews and the Arab people to live in peace.

I am publishing about sixty books a year, so each author on my list may have one book a year. I feel a responsibility to authors to keep their books in print as long as possible. I personally keep books in print for longer than I should with the economics of today. The advent of ebooks might, with the help of Amazon, make a big change. It's hard to assess. However, I believe most dedicated readers want a book in their hand, rather than a piece of plastic.

Jackie and I take a lot more time off lately and I guess it will be the beginning of a slow exit from the business. We enjoy being part-time grey nomads in our camper van. I'm now sixty-four years of age and try not to think about mortality. But it creeps up, especially when I catch a breath or I hear Mum talking to me from beyond that veil.

And now there's another anxiety. Jillian is on the nightly news in the bloody Balkans. A journo, a war correspondent, do you mind. Wearing her vest, which hides the flat left side where a breast was removed. Her blonde ponytail and Dad's eyes pierce onto the screen with the sounds of war too close for comfort.

Her last phone call was about her new love. 'No, the stunt man shot through once the breast went west. Just ego. No real substance. I'm with Ivan, a tragic Russian concert pianist, who makes me laugh a lot. We're off to Russia very soon. Love to Jackie. Bye.'

And I was left wondering about her life. Perhaps she takes after me. God keep her safe.

Author's Note

The characters in this story are all fictitious and any resemblance to anyone, in or out of my life, is not intentional. The chapters regarding the navy in 1956 relate only to my observations as a reservist, during my national service, at sea and at the Flinders Naval Depot in Victoria.

It's all history now, concerning the bullying, character assassinations and sexual abuse during initiation ceremonies (which were not restricted to the armed services). I underwent a couple of those so-called 'make a man out of you' incidents when I was an apprentice at the Municipal Tramways Trust in Hackney, South Australia. One of the boys committed suicide some time later, after his ordeal at the hands of older tradesmen. So there's more than a ring of truth in the scene I've written in the story.

The worst kept secret in the navy was 'no gays'. Funny about that, as I met quite a few of them, who served with distinction in spite of their sexual predilections. Hypocrisy just doesn't go away.

The Korean War ended in 1953; however, the logistics of returning to homelands took some time to implement. Accordingly, the United Nations and countries involved were not able to commence a total withdrawal until the end of 1954. Some RAN ships were still in the Korean peninsula area until the end of 1955. Complicating the withdrawal plans were offensive operations during the war in Malaya, a zone close to Korea.

www.ingramcontent.com/pod-product-compliance
Lightning Source LLC
Chambersburg PA
CBHW020347110726
47898CB00003B/1074